For Ard, with admiration and gratitude
—M. C.

To my visionary friend Jessica Handelman, with great appreciation
—A. H.

SIMON & SCHUSTER BOOKS FOR YOUNG READERS

An imprint of Simon & Schuster Children's Publishing Division

1230 Avenue of the Americas, New York, New York 10020

Text copyright © 2011 by Mary Casanova · Illustrations copyright © 2011 by Ard Hoyt

All rights reserved, including the right of reproduction in whole or in part in any form.

SIMON & SCHUSTER BOOKS FOR YOUNG READERS is a trademark of Simon & Schuster, Inc.

For information about special discounts for bulk purchases, please contact Simon &

Schuster Special Sales at 1-866-506-1949 or business@simonandschuster.com.

The Simon & Schuster Speakers Bureau can bring authors to your live event.

For more information or to book an event, contact the Simon & Schuster Speakers

Bureau at 1-866-248-3049 or visit our website at www.simonspeakers.com.

Book design by Jessica Handelman · The text for this book is set in Venetian.

The illustrations for this book are rendered in pen and ink.

Manufactured in China · 0811 SCP · 10 9 8 7 6 5 4 3 2 1

Library of Congress Cataloging-in-Publication Data

Casanova, Mary.

Utterly otterly night / Mary Casanova ; illustrated by Ard Hoyt.— · 1st ed. · p. cm.

Summary: While out playing with his family one night, Little Otter shows that he knows

what to do when danger is near.

ISBN 978-1-4169-7562-5 · [1. Otters—Fiction.] I. Hoyt, Ard, ill. II. Title.

PZ7.C266Uv 2011 · [E]—dc22 · 2010026429

BY Mary Casanova   PICTURES BY Ard Hoyt

Utterly Otterly Night

SIMON & SCHUSTER BOOKS FOR YOUNG READERS · New York · London · Toronto · Sydney

Down below the river's ceiling,
underneath earth's snowy blanket,
Little Otter's ready to play,
in an utterly otterly way.

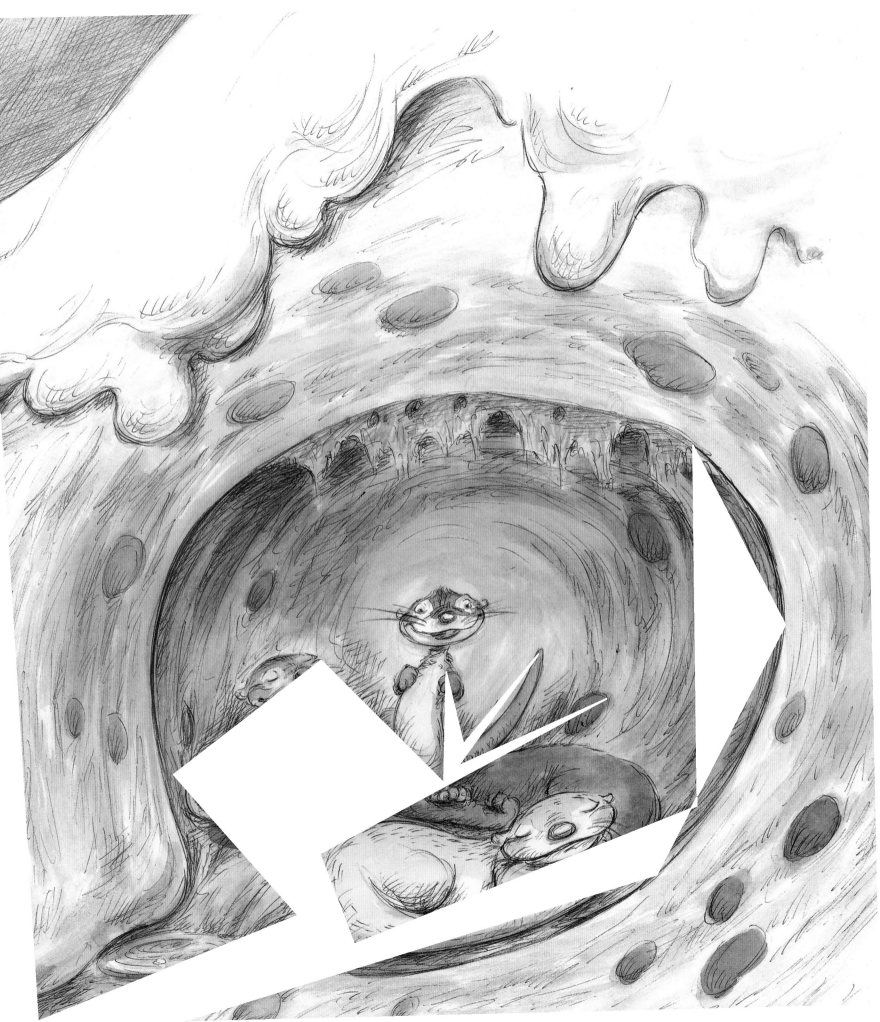

He tickles Sister's paws,
then nudges Papa's chin.
"Let's go," Mama chirps.
"But first hint of danger—
we *all* head in."

Little Otter pops
through a hole in the ice,
to a glimmery, shimmery
moonlit night.

He's a big otter now—
he knows what to do!

To the crest of the hill,
Little Otter bounds,
then drops to his belly—

friskily, whiskily down.

With a *whoomping* of feet,
an explosion of white,
Rabbit bursts
from her winter bed—
right over Little Otter's head!

Up and down, the otters play.
They glide and slide,

in a whooshily,

"Watch out!" Papa cries.
Owl swoops low . . .
Little Otter plows . . .

Puffy, fluffy snow!

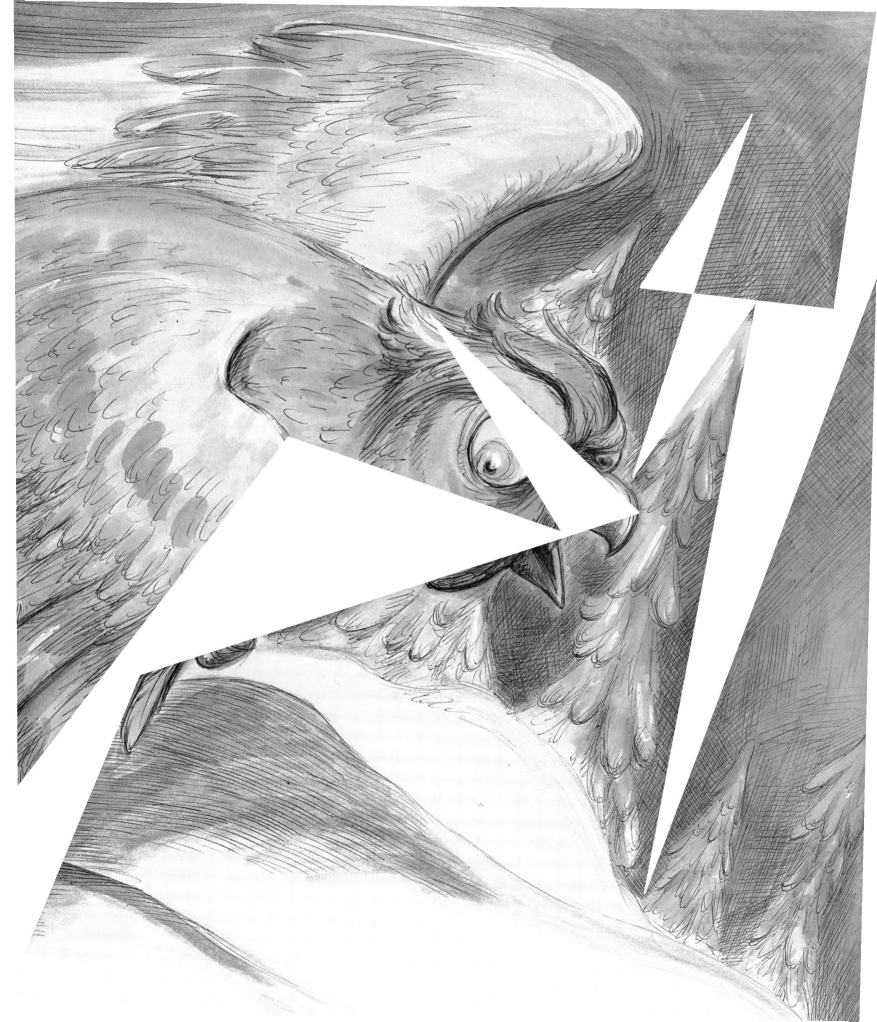

In a flurry of flakes,
he's back at the top.

whiz, glide, a speedy ride!

Halfway down—he puts on his brakes—
almost too late!
Moose towers.
Little Otter cowers.

Then—chompity,
whompity,
STOMP—

off Moose clomps.

Little Otter scampers
to a higher snowtop
delightfully, then *oh* . . .
so frightfully
slows to a stop.

He lifts his head toward leafless trees.
He smells *trouble* on the breeze.
Little Otter's feeling grows.
Little Otter *knows* he knows.

"Danger!" he cries.
But his family can't hear.
They slide and play,
in an utterly otterly way.

Peering out from piney shadows,
big teeth . . . big eyes . . .

one . . .

two . . .

Heart bump-bumping,
Little Otter circles wide,
pretending to play

in a quakingly, shakingly way.

He's a big otter now.
He knows what to do.
Little Otter hopes they'll follow.
Little Otter *fears* they'll swallow!

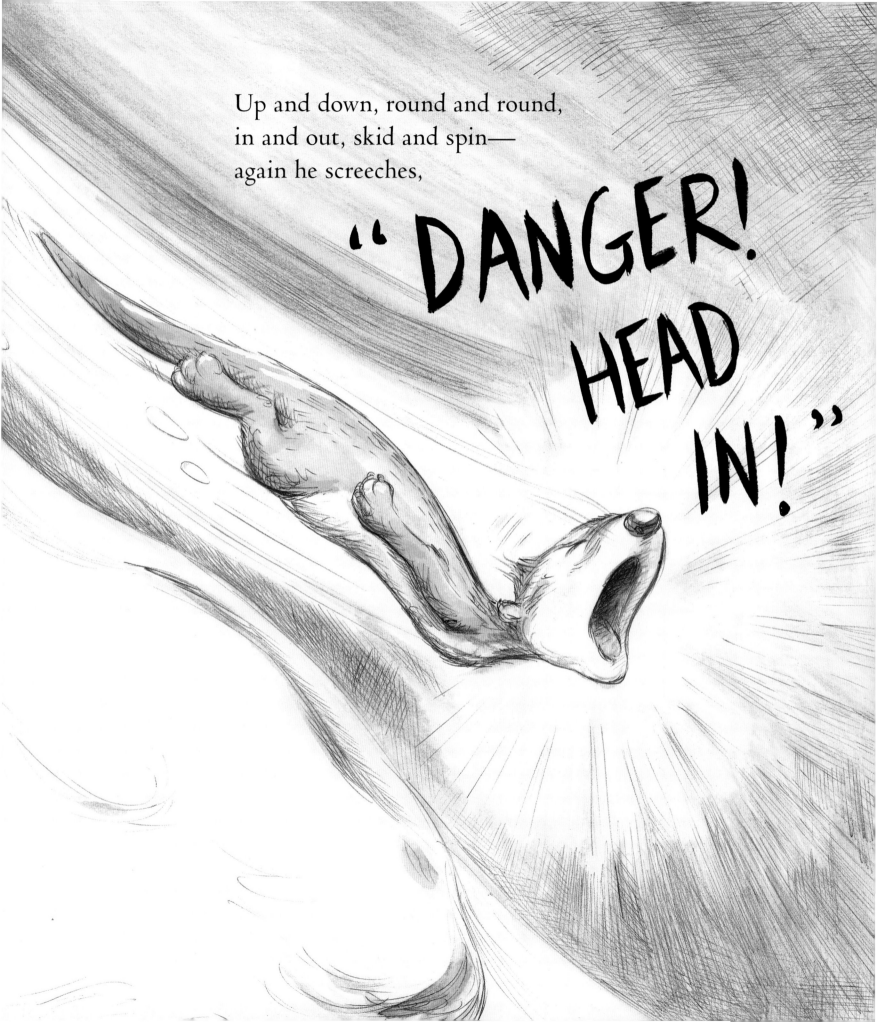

Up and down, round and round,
in and out, skid and spin—
again he screeches,

"DANGER!
HEAD
IN!"

Now his family hears his warning,
slides toward river's open water,
and icily, dicily
disappears.

A growl!
He flops!

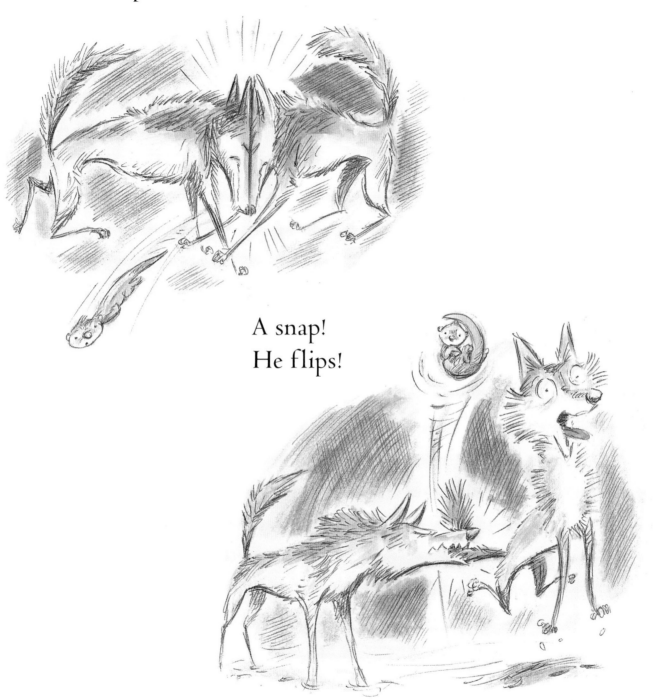

A snap!
He flips!

And slips right through!

Back inside his safe, snug den,
Little Otter grooms and preens—
Mama, Papa, Sister, too—
licking, cleaning, drying fur,
just as otters do.

Down below the river's ceiling,
underneath earth's snowy blanket,
all is right
on a friskily, whiskily,
whooshily, shooshily,
icily, dicily,
frightfully, delightfully,

utterly otterly night.